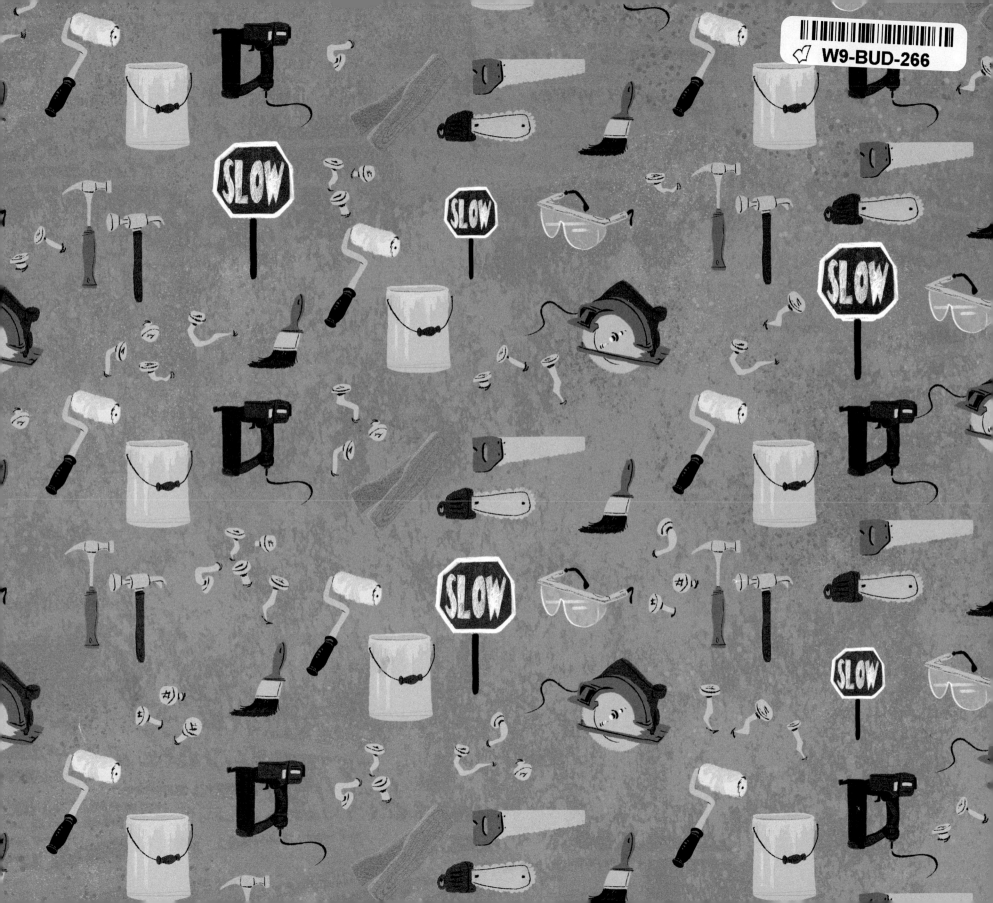

For my son Finn, who is often found in our garage
searching for tools to dismantle his toys! –S. G.

For my husband, Dax, who is always fixing something
in our home with his tools.–E. K.

Book design by Ryan Hayes.
Typeset in Bandoliers, Monstro, and Populaire.
Illustrations in this book were rendered in pencil and
gouache, and composited digitally.

10 9 8 7 6 5 4 3 2 1

Chronicle Books LLC
680 Second Street
San Francisco, California 94107

Chronicle Books—we see things differently. Become part of
our community at www.chroniclekids.com.

OLD MacDONALD
HAD A BOAT

By
Steve Goetz

Illustrated by
Eda Kaban

chronicle books · san francisco

Old MacDonald had a farm
E-I-E-I-O.

DOCK
HOME
ARENA
SAN FRANCISCO
BARN

And on that farm he had a . . .

E - I - E - I - O.
With a **SLOW SLOW** here
and a **SLOW SLOW** there,

here a SLOW, there a SLOW,
everywhere a SLOW SLOW.

Old MacDonald had a farm
E - I - E - I - O.
And on that farm he had a . . .

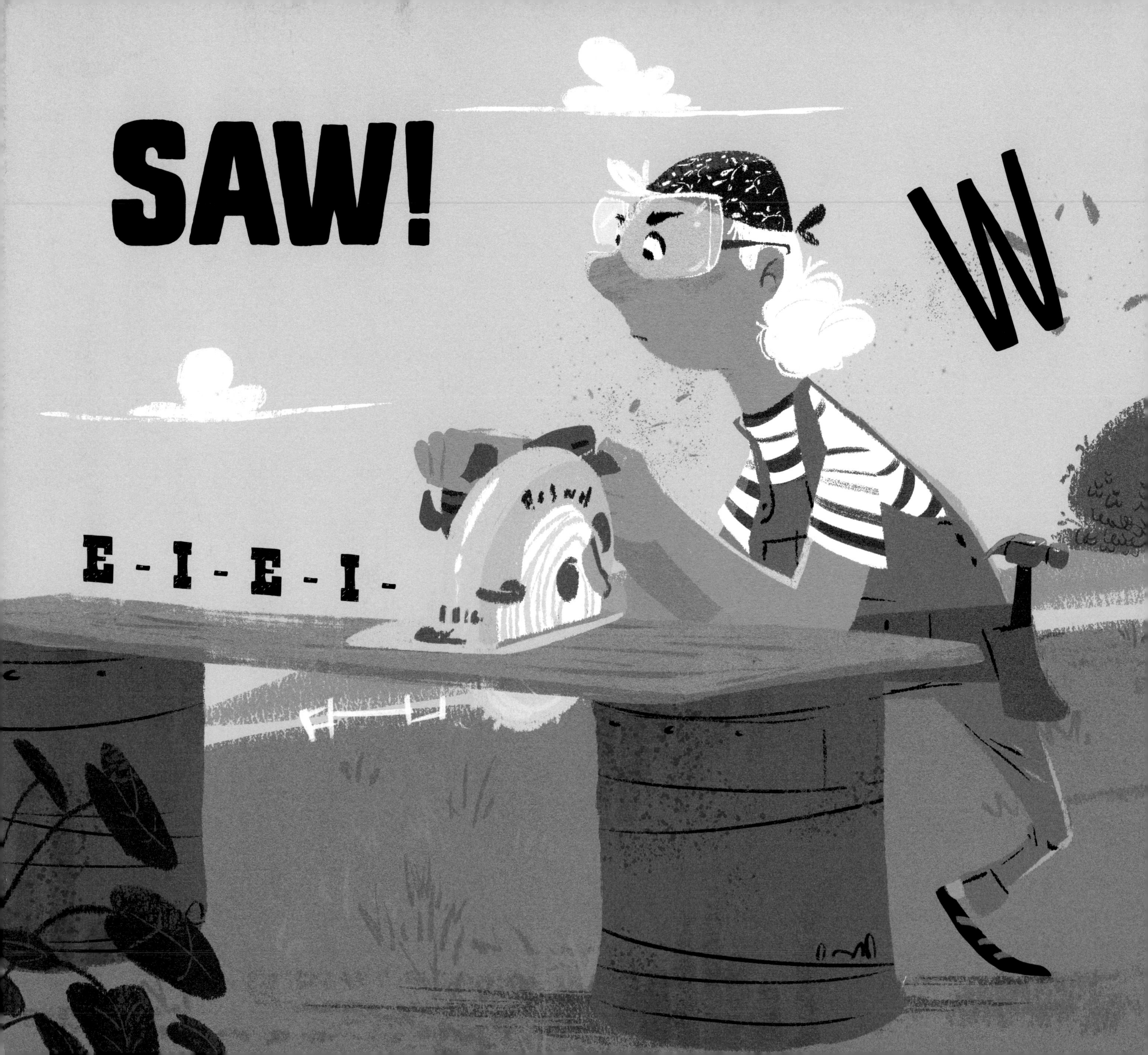
SAW!
E-I-E-I-
W

HOA!

With a **BUZZ BUZZ** here
and a **BUZZ BUZZ** there,

Old MacDonald had a farm
E - I - E - I - O.
And on that farm he had a . . .

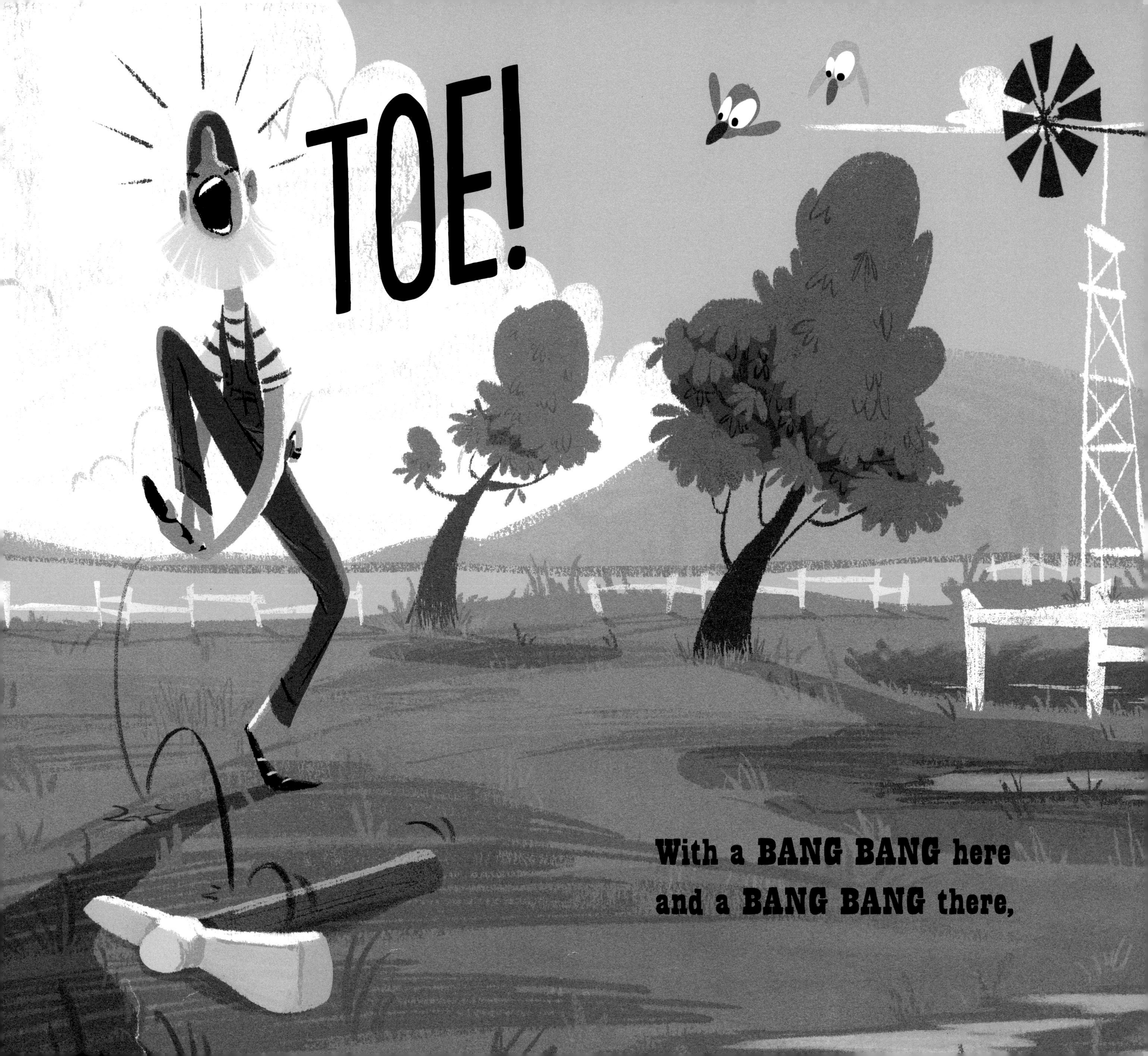

With a **BANG BANG** here
and a **BANG BANG** there,

here a **BANG**, there a **BANG**,
everywhere a **BANG BANG**.

Old MacDonald had a farm
E - I - E - I - O.

And on that farm he had a . . .

here a BLOW, there a BLOW,
everywhere a BLOW BLOW.

Old MacDonald had a farm
E - I - E - I - O.
And on that farm he had a . . .

SHHH- SHHH-OH!

With a SHHH-SHHH here
and a SHHH-SHHH there,

here a SHHH, there a SHHH,
everywhere a SHHH-SHHH.

Old MacDonald had a farm
E - I - E - I - O.
And on that farm he had a . . .

E-I-E-I- GLOW!

With a ROLL ROLL here
and a ROLL ROLL there,

here a **ROLL**, there a **ROLL**,
everywhere a **ROLL ROLL**.

Old MacDonald had a farm
E - I - E - I - O.
And on that farm he had a . . .

here a SPLISH, there a SPLASH,
everywhere a SPLISH SPLASH.

Old MacDonald had a farm
E - I - E - I - O.
And on that farm he had a . . .